THERE'S A
DRAGON
IN MY SLEEPING BAG

THERE'S A
DRAGON
IN MY SLEEPING BAG

by James Howe   illustrated by David S. Rose

Aladdin Paperbacks

First Aladdin Paperbacks edition May 1998

Aladdin Paperbacks
An imprint of Simon & Schuster
Children's Publishing Division
1230 Avenue of the Americas
New York, NY 10020

Also available in an Atheneum Books for Young Readers hardcover edition.

The text of this book is set in Korinna.
The illustrations are rendered in acrylics.

Manufactured in China
10 9 8 7

The Library of Congress has cataloged the hardcover edition as follows:
Howe, James, 1946-
There's a dragon in my sleeping bag / by James Howe :
illustrated by David S. Rose. — 1st ed.
p.   cm.
Summary: Alex is intimidated by his older brother Simon's imaginary dragon,
until he is able to create his own friend—a camel named Calvin.
ISBN 0-689-31873-1 (hc)
[1. Brothers—Fiction. 2. Imaginary playmates—Fiction.]
I. Rose, David S., 1947-   ill. II. Title.
PZ7.H83727Tg   1994
[E]—dc20   93-26572
ISBN-13: 978-0-689-81922-3 (Aladdin pbk.)
ISBN-10: 0-689-81922-6 (Aladdin pbk.)

To Zoey
and our friend Calvin
—J. H.

To Apple
—D. S. R.

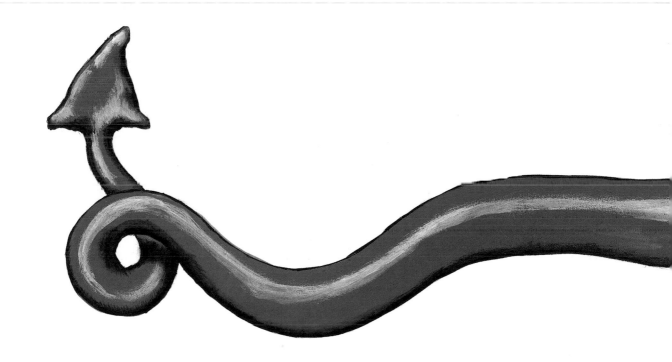

There's a dragon in my sleeping bag. I can't see him, but my brother says he's there.

"You'll have to sleep somewhere else tonight,"
Simon tells me. "If you lie down on top of Dexter,
he'll breathe fire on you and you'll look funny without
any hair."

I sleep on the floor.

At breakfast, there's a dragon in my chair.

"Don't sit there," Simon says, "or Dexter will
breathe fire and burn your bagel."

I hate burned bagels, so I sit in Dad's chair instead.

When I go outside to play, Simon tells me there's a dragon on my swing...

on my end of the seesaw…

and stuck in the middle of the slide.

"I'm going inside," I tell Simon. "It's no fun out here."

But Simon doesn't answer me. He's too busy laughing at something with Dexter.

It used to be just Simon and me. But since this dragon Dexter came to live at our house, Simon doesn't want to play with me anymore.

"I'll play with you."
"Who said that?" I ask.
"My name is Calvin."
"You're a camel."
"It's nice of you to notice," Calvin says. "Want to play?"

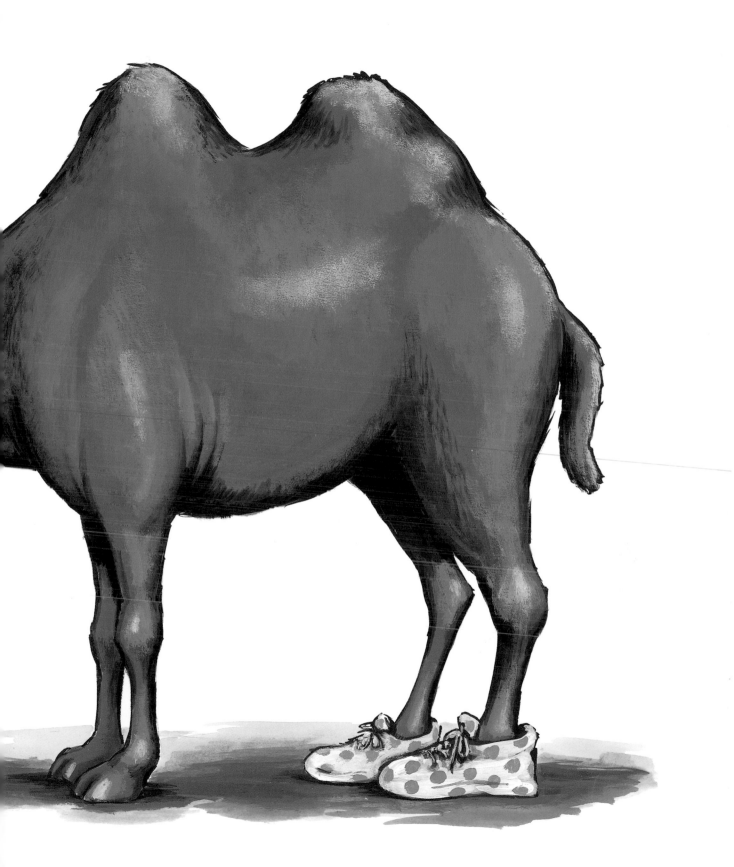

I tell Calvin yes, and the best thing happens. Calvin likes to play the same games I do. And he always lets me win.

Not like Simon.

"You can't sleep there," I tell Simon that night.
"Why not?" Simon asks.
"Because there's a camel in your sleeping bag."
Simon can't see Calvin just like I can't see Dexter.
He gives me a dirty look, but he doesn't say
anything.

In the morning, I tell him, "Sorry, Simon, you'll have to sit somewhere else. That's Calvin's seat and if you sit on top of him he'll breathe camel breath on you."

When we go outside to play,

both swings are busy....

ro
se

the
wh
mi
S
mu
mo
got

That night, we have to put two more chairs at the table. "My," Mom says, "if I'd known we were going to have so much company for dinner, I would have roasted a larger chicken."

"That's okay," I tell her. "Calvin is a vegetarian."
Everyone laughs at that.
Everyone but Simon.

"This is supposed to be fun," I tell Calvin. "Why are you so down in the dumps? Don't you like riding with me?"

"Sure," Calvin says. "It's just…well, I miss someone."

"Oh," is all I say, because I have to use the rest of my breath for pedaling up a hill.

"What are you doing?" Simon asks when I drag my sleeping bag into his room that night.

"I'm going to sleep in here with you."

"But what about Calvin?"

"He's gone," I say. "He left a note. See?

"'Dear Alex. I have moved to Boston. I will miss you but I miss Dexter more. That's the way it is with best friends. Goodbye. Calvin.'"

Simon nods. "Well, at least we don't have to worry about camel breath anymore."

"Yep," I say. "Or dragon breath, either."

"Good night, Alex."

"Good night, Simon."

"You know what, Alex? I feel sorry for Dexter and Calvin."

"You do? Why?"

"Because they're only best friends, but we're brothers."

"Yeah," I say. "Hey, Simon."

"What?"

"Will you play with me tomorrow?"

"Of course, Alex. After all, what's a brother for?"